DC SUPER FRIENDS™

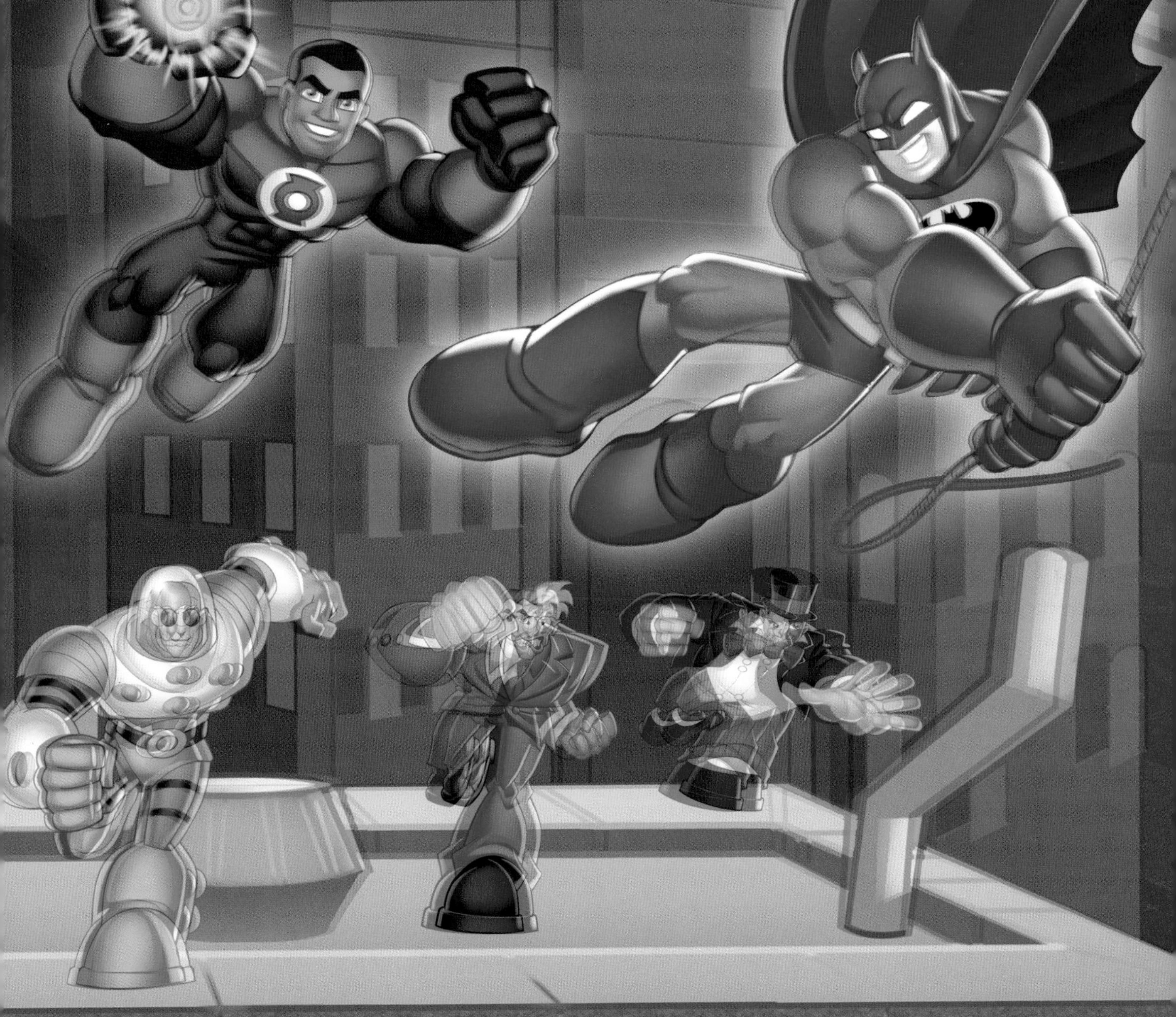

BIG AND BOLD!

By D. R. Shealy

A GOLDEN BOOK • NEW YORK

 Published in the United States by Golden Books, an imprint of Random House Children's Books, a division of Random House, Inc., 1745 Broadway, New York, NY 10019, and in Canada by Random House of Canada Limited, Toronto. Golden Books, A Golden Book, and the G colophon are registered trademarks of Random House, Inc.

ISBN: 978-0-375-84746-2 www.randomhouse.com/kids MANUFACTURED IN CHINA

10 9 8 7 6 5 4 3 2 1

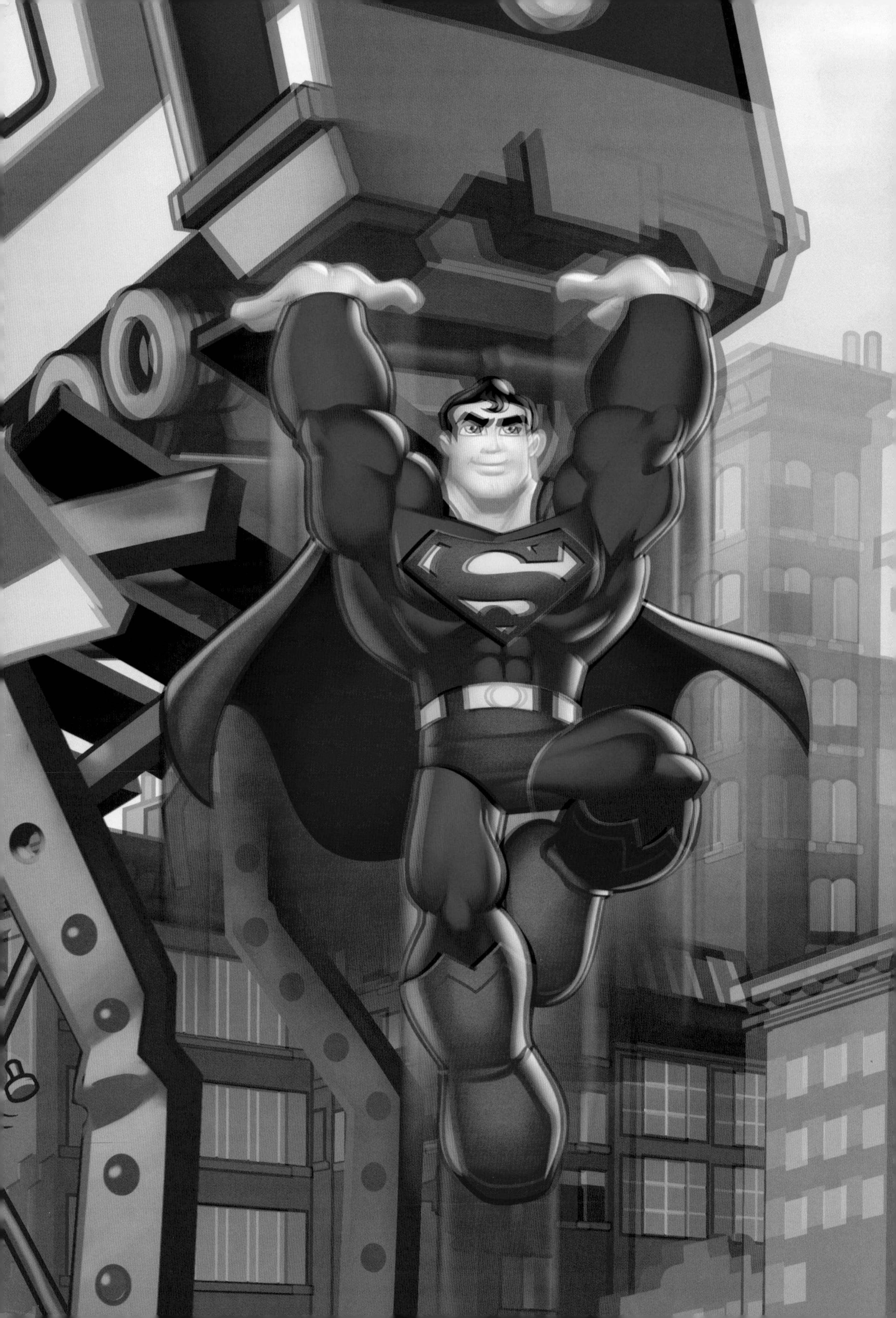

SUPERMAN

The Man of Steel uses his amazing superpowers for good! He has super-strength, and he can fly at super-speed. Superman's super-cold breath can put the chill on the bad guys, and his heat vision can cut through any substance.

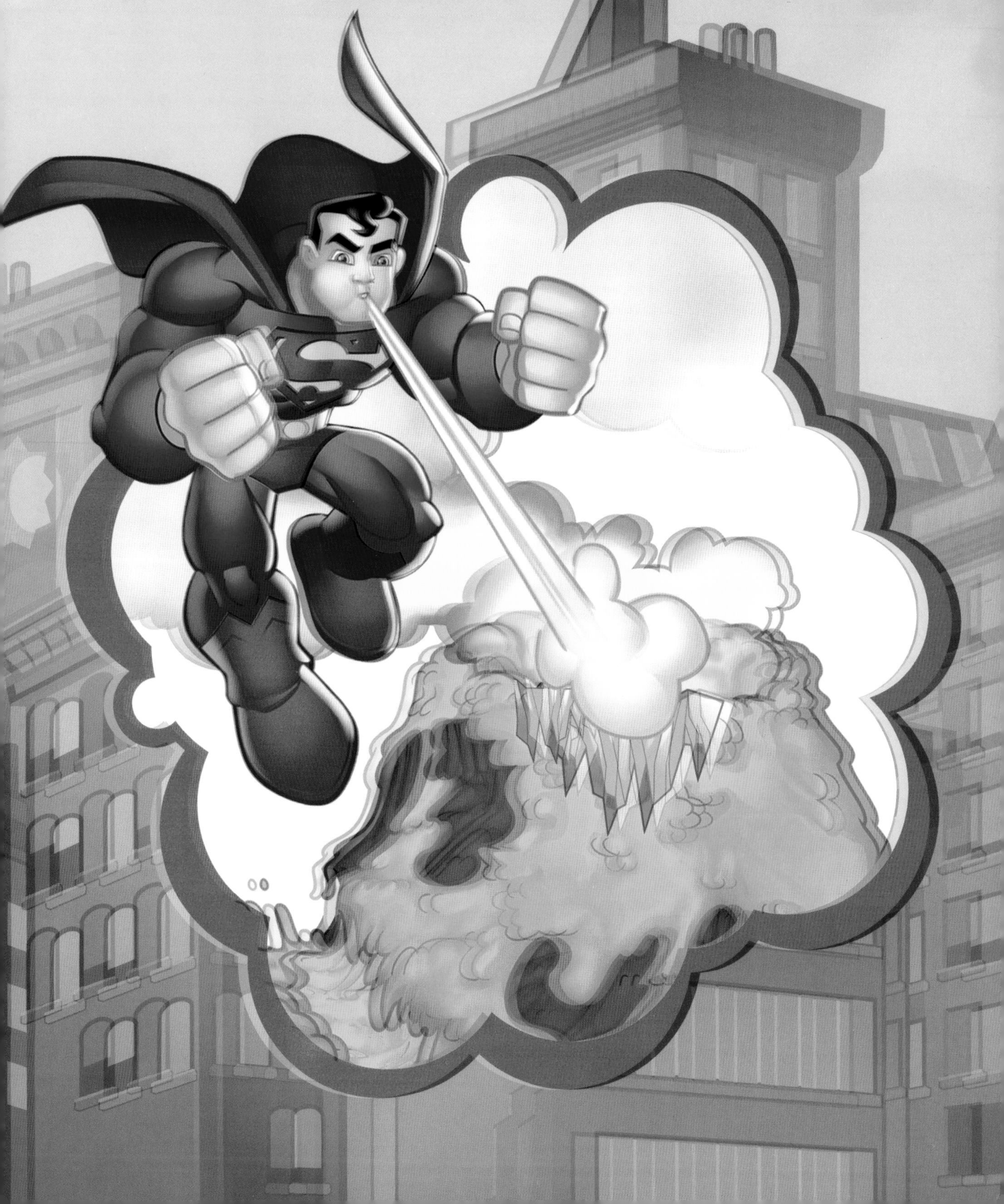

THE FLASH

The Flash is the Fastest Man Alive. He moves so fast that he can run up walls and across water!

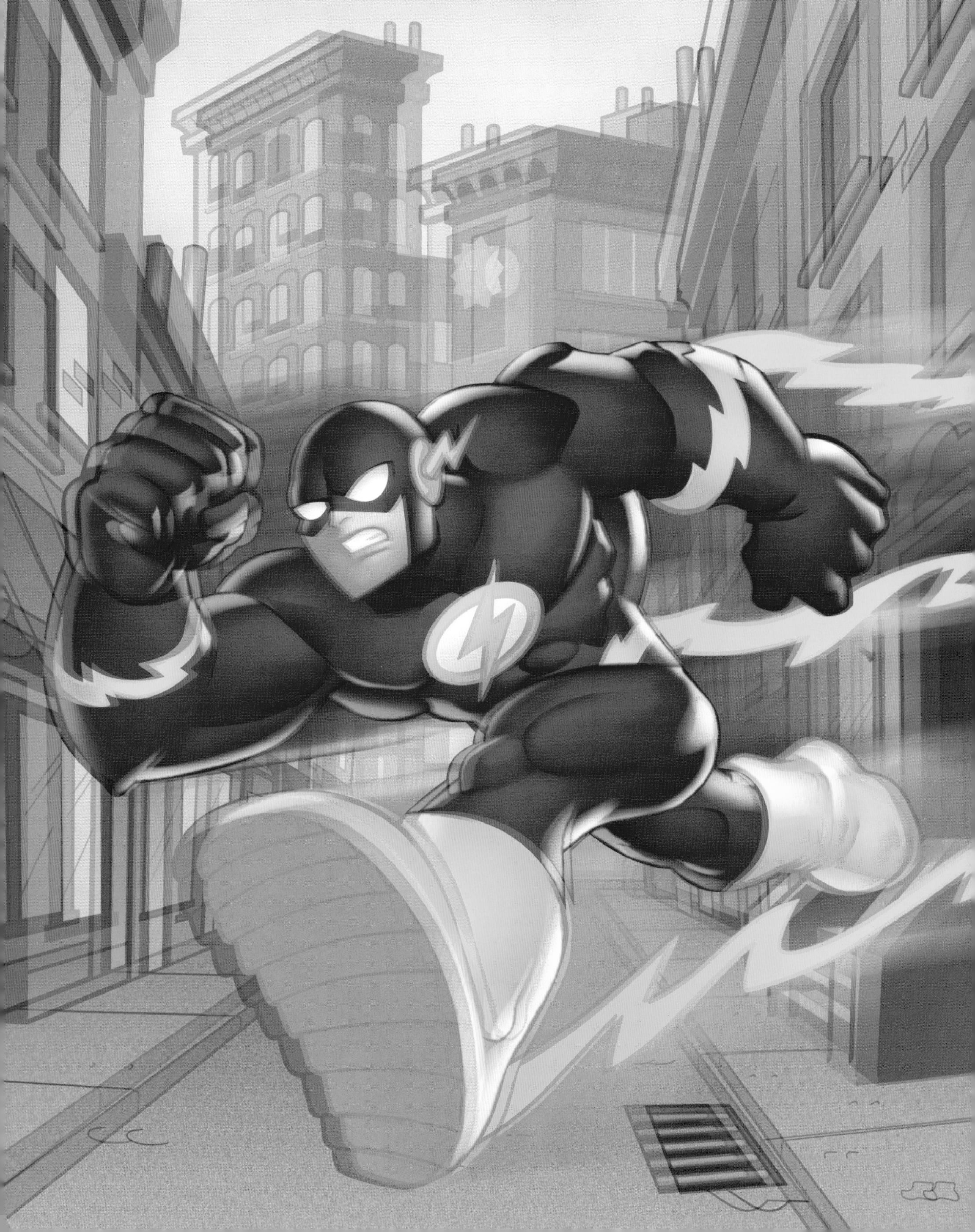

GREEN LANTERN

The Galactic Guardian can do anything with his glowing green Power Ring. He uses his ring to fly, generate indestructible force fields, and create any object he can imagine!

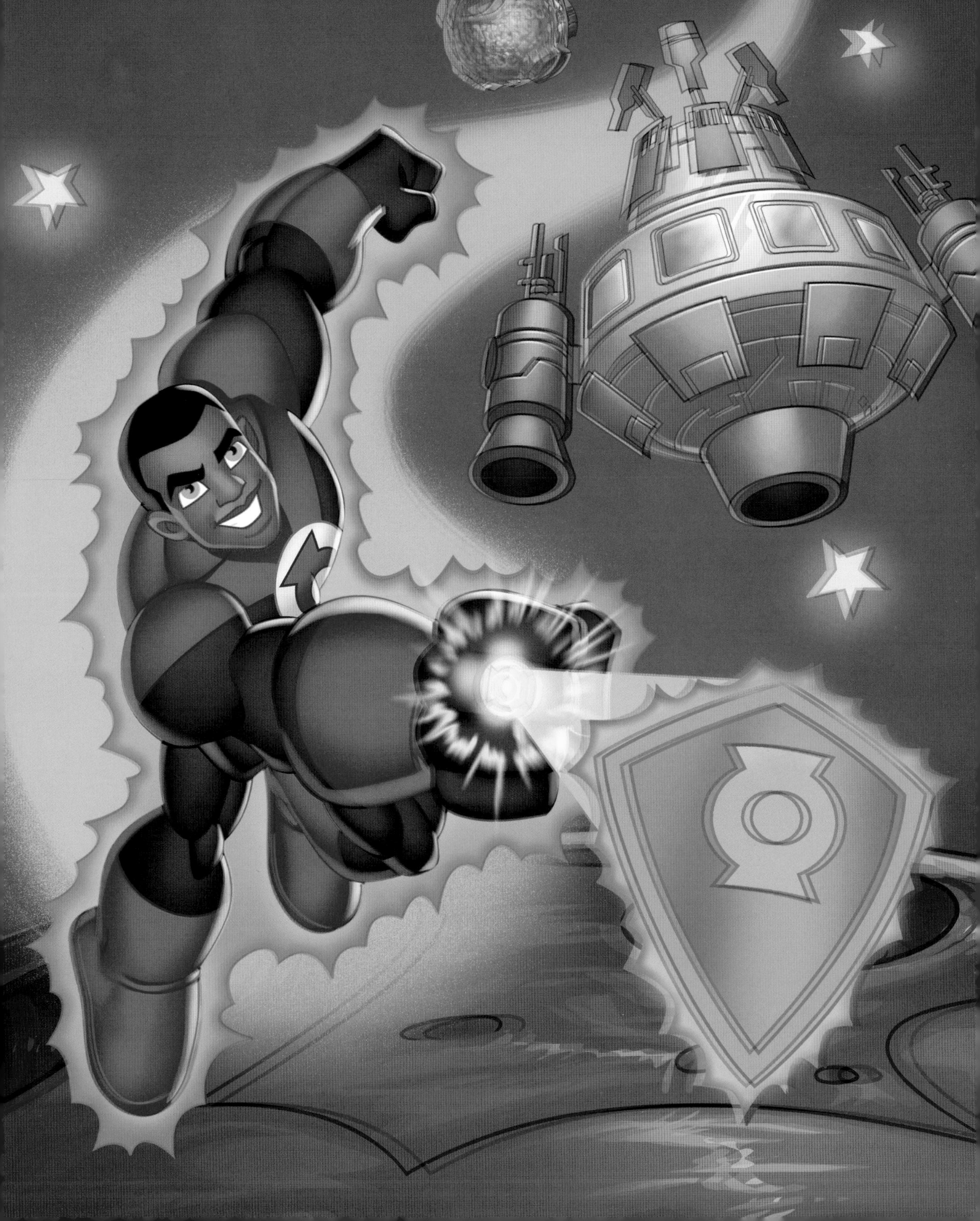

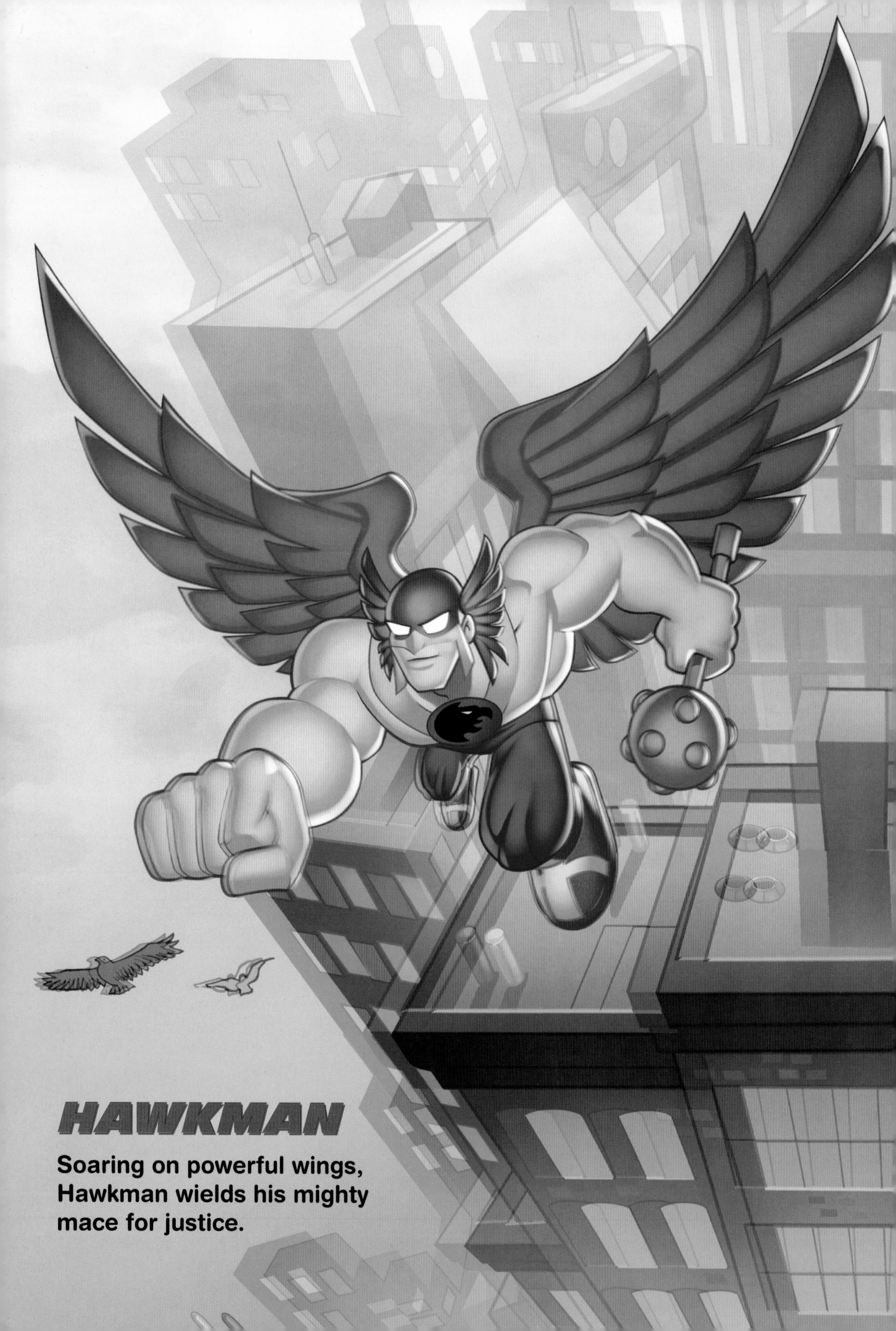

HAWKMAN

Soaring on powerful wings,
Hawkman wields his mighty
mace for justice.

Cyborg is half man, half machine. This young hero can transform his arm into many different technological tools. His machine body makes him super-strong.

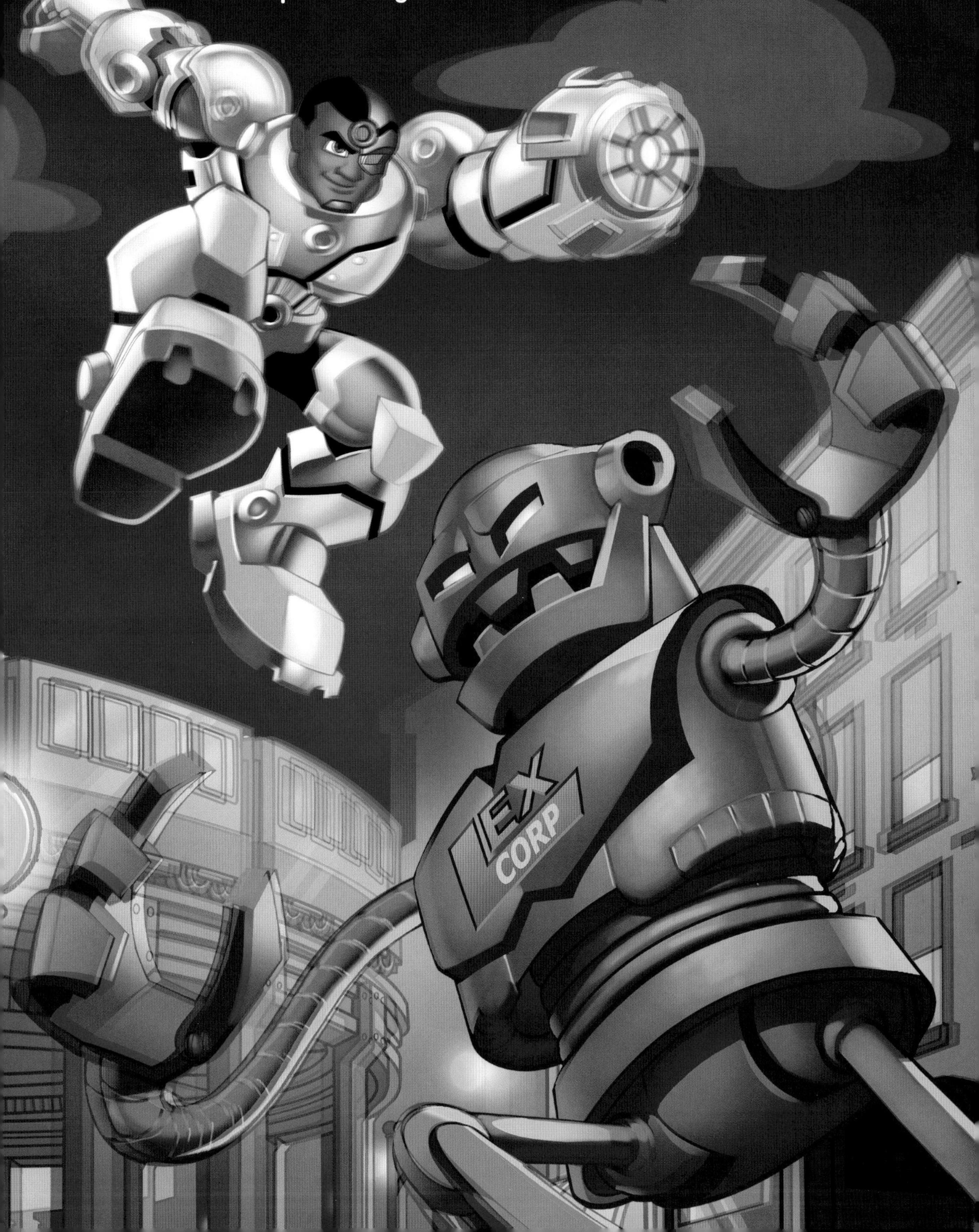
EX
CORP

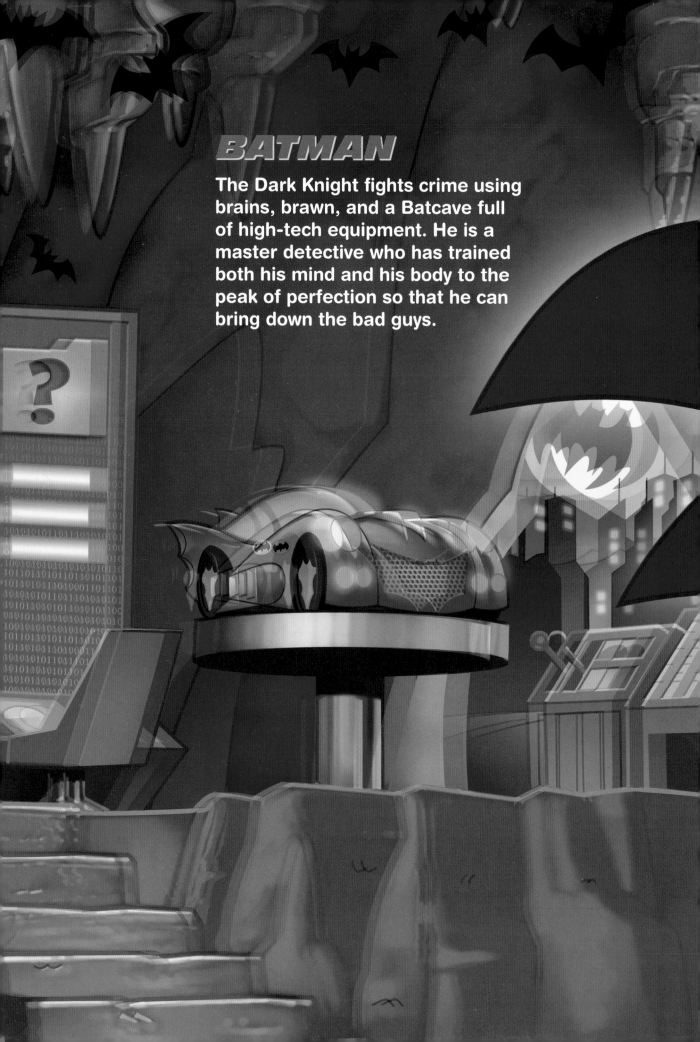

BATMAN

The Dark Knight fights crime using brains, brawn, and a Batcave full of high-tech equipment. He is a master detective who has trained both his mind and his body to the peak of perfection so that he can bring down the bad guys.

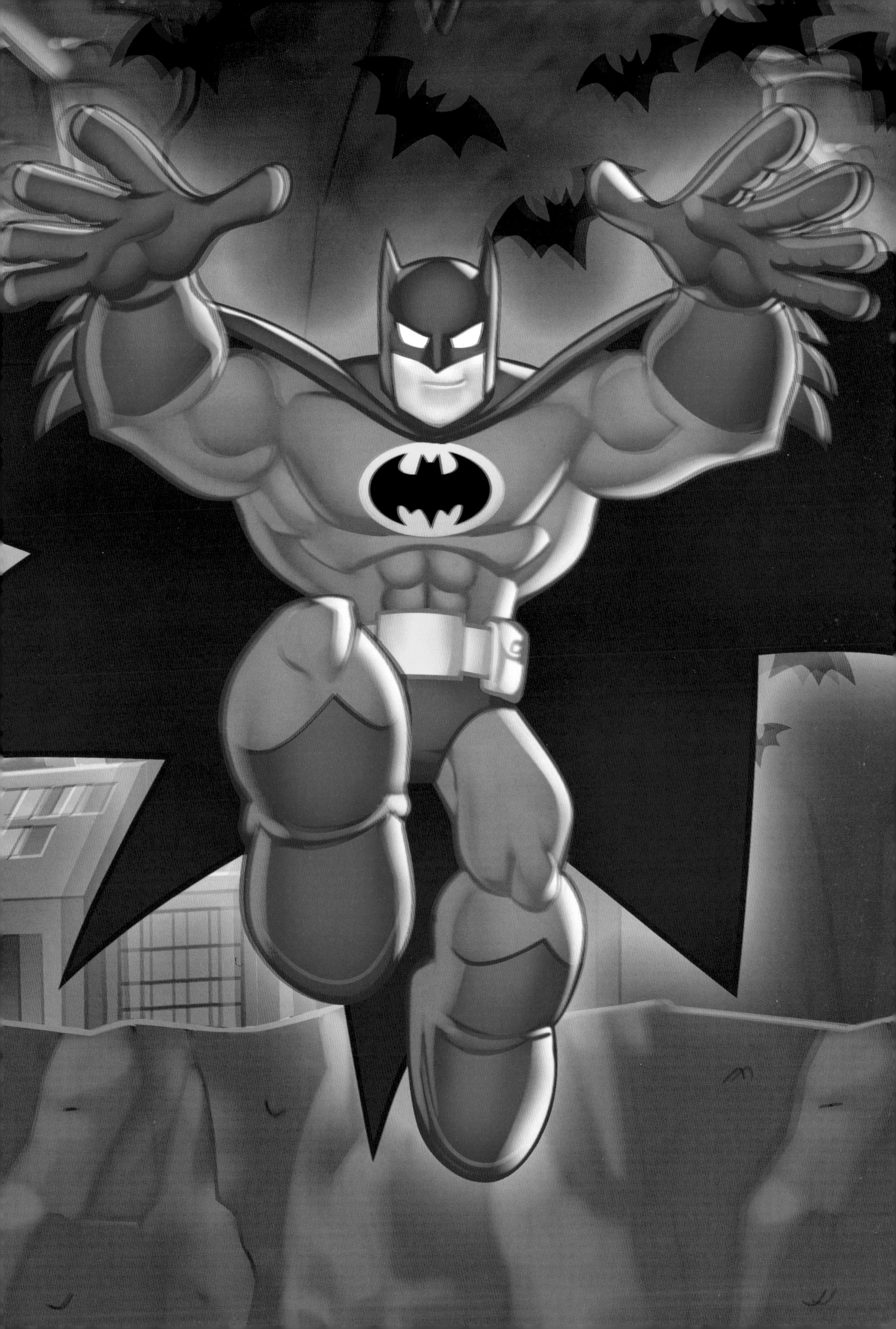

ROBIN

Batman's sidekick, the Boy Wonder,
is always ready to swing into action.
Robin has been trained by Batman
to be an amazing crime fighter!

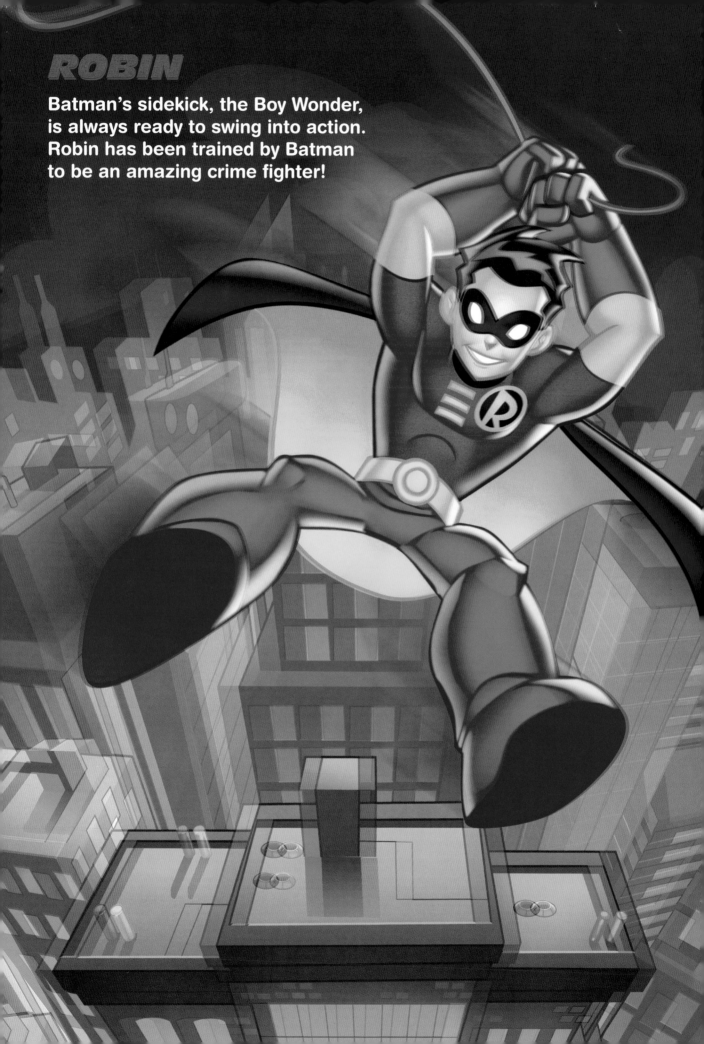

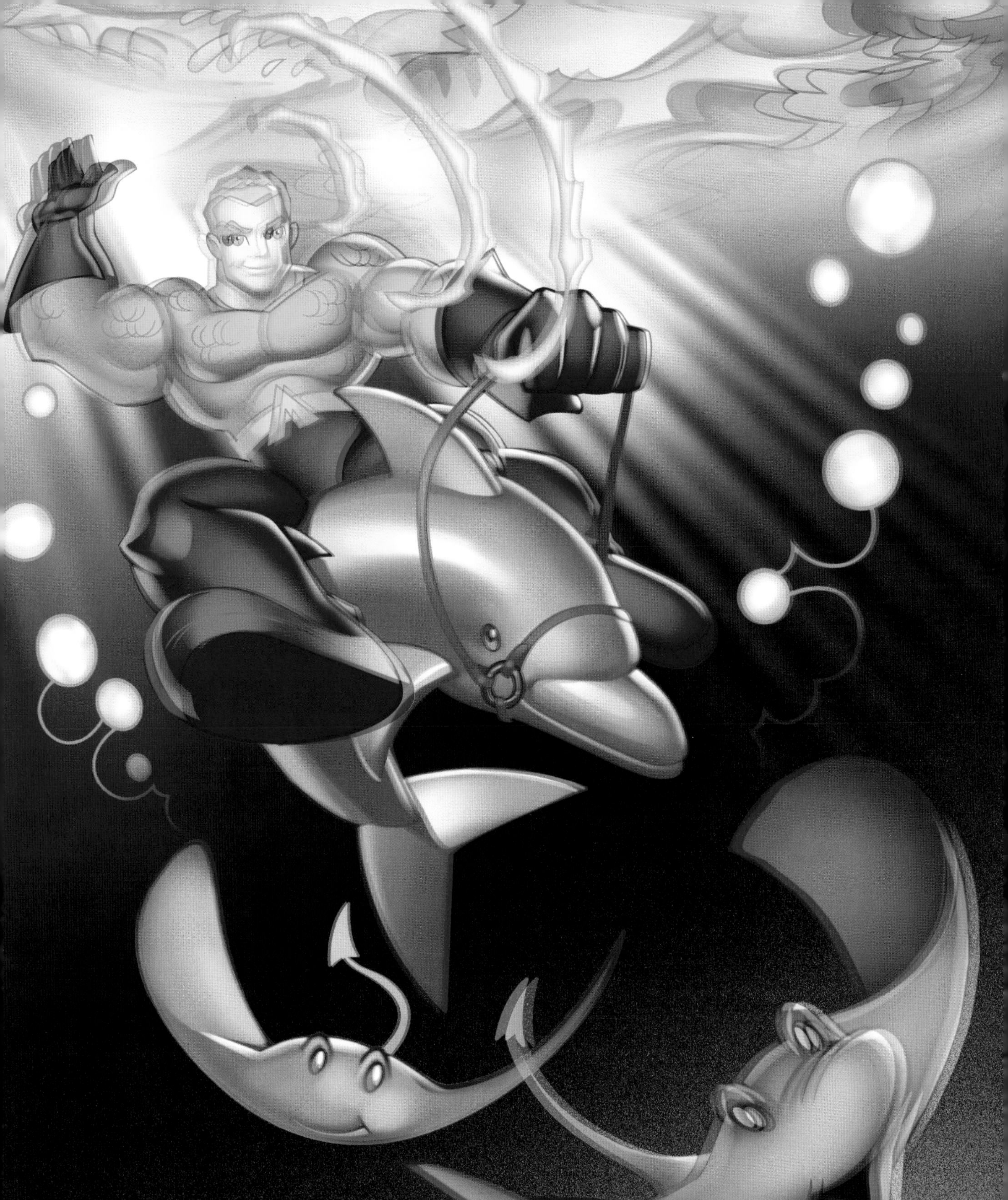

AQUAMAN

The deep-diving King of Atlantis can communicate with all of the ocean's creatures. He calls upon them to protect humankind from aquatic threats.

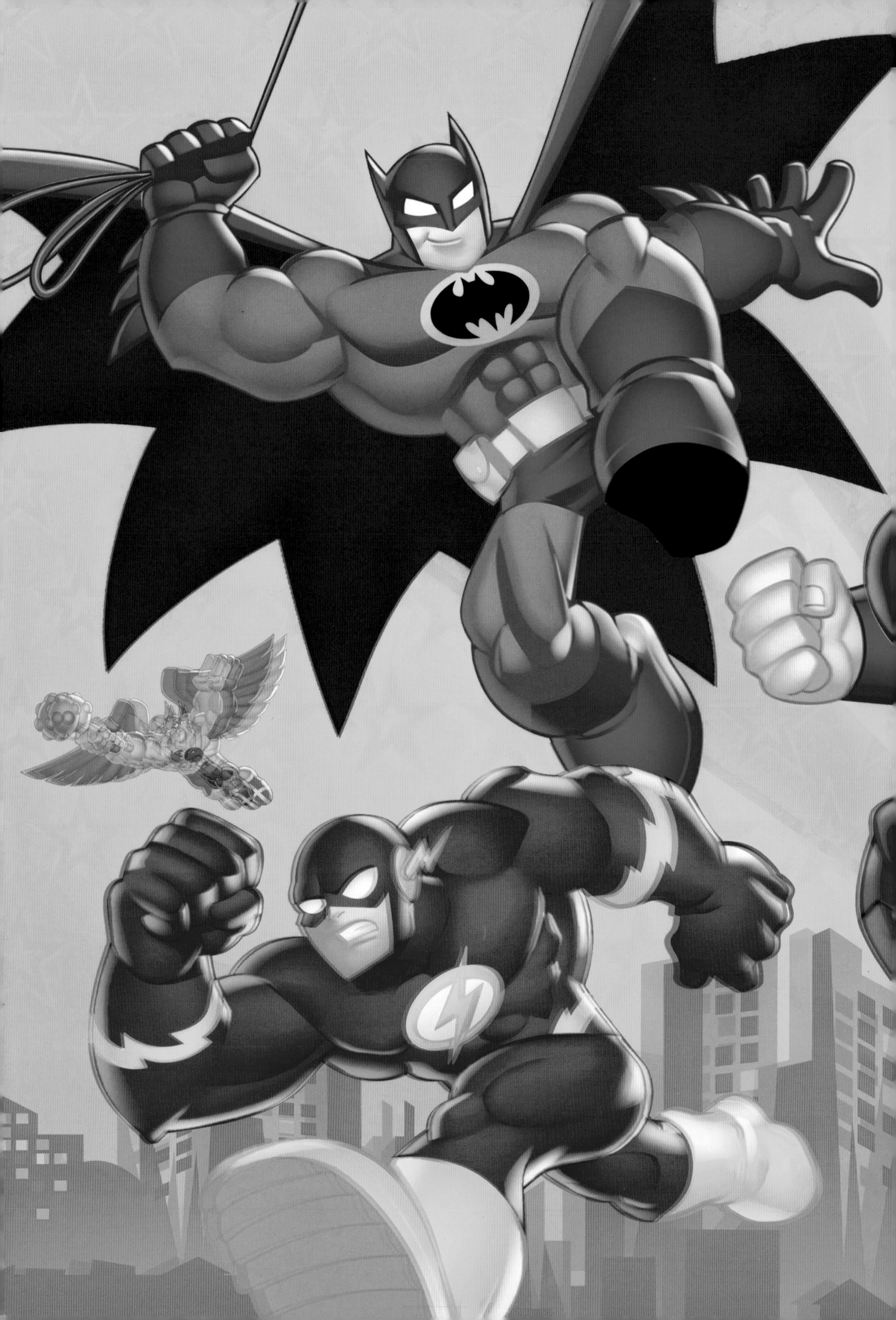

THE SUPER FRIENDS

Together, these mighty heroes are unstoppable!

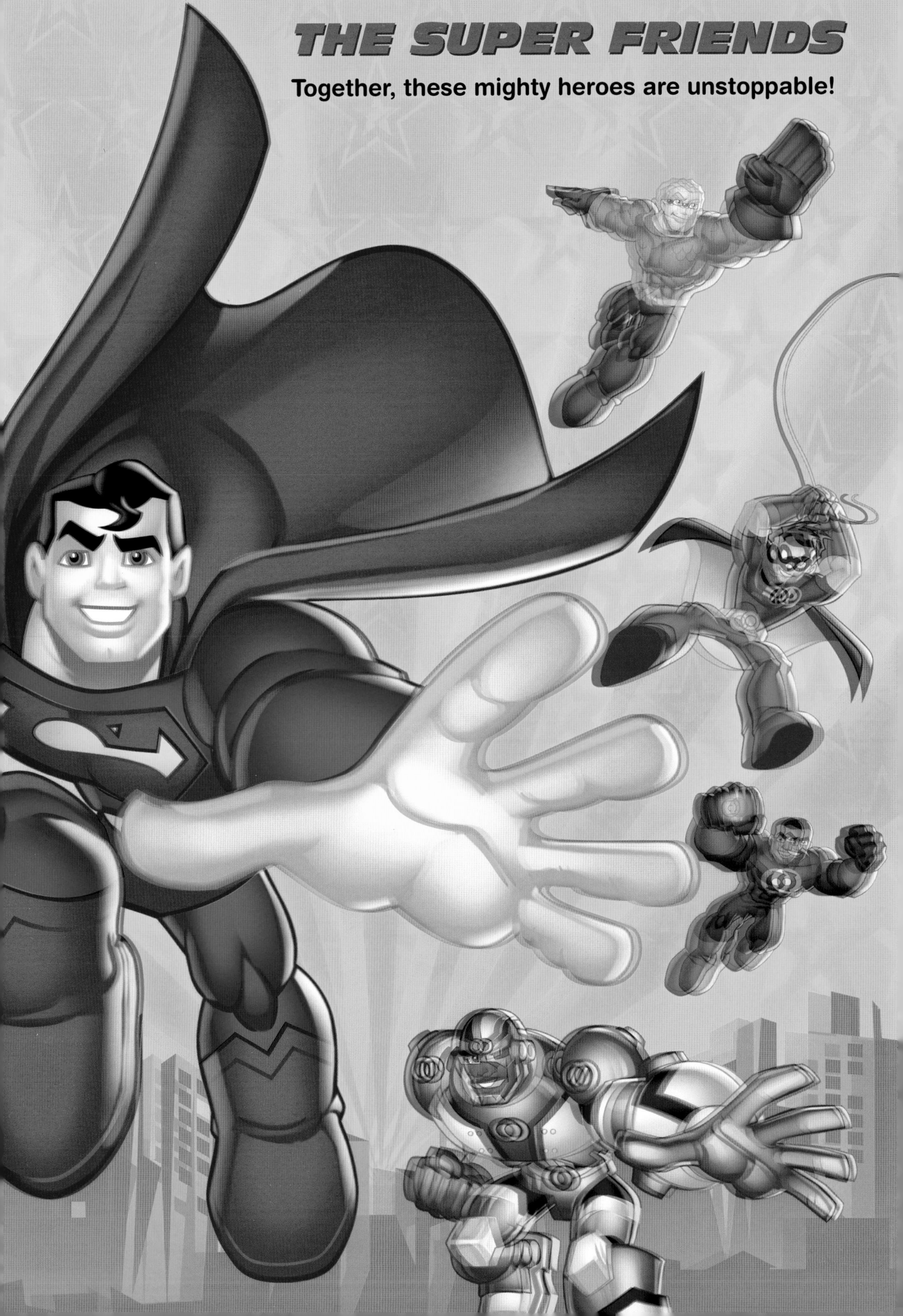

THE RIDDLER • THE JOKER

The Riddler likes to leave clues to his crimes, and the Joker thinks it's funny to be a wisecracking crook. It's too bad for them that Batman and the other Super Friends always put a stop to their criminal capers!

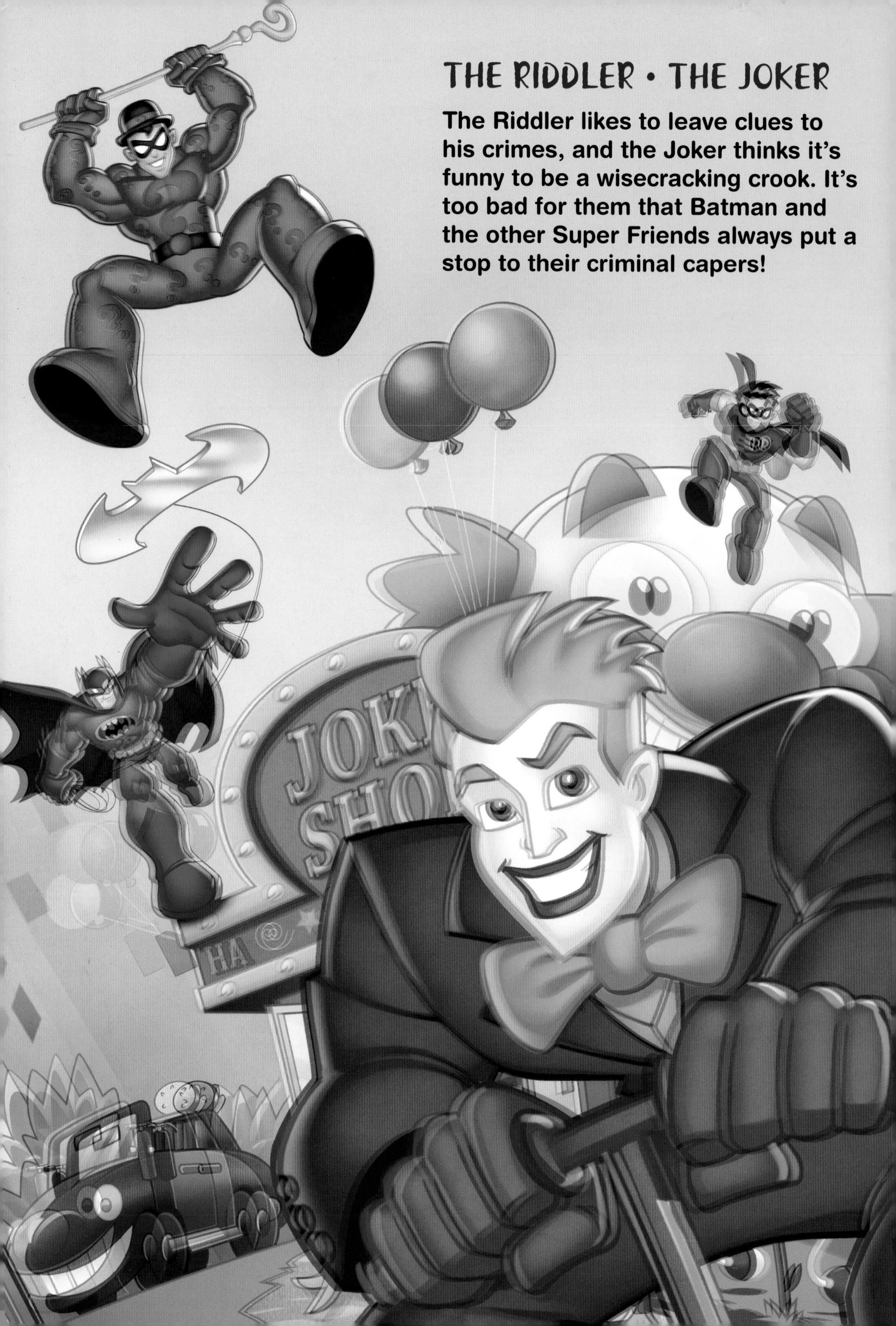
HA

THE PENGUIN • MR. FREEZE

The Penguin is a bad bird who uses a deadly umbrella to swoop down on the Super Friends. Brrr . . . Mr. Freeze's armor creates blasts of cold that are as frosty as his evil heart.

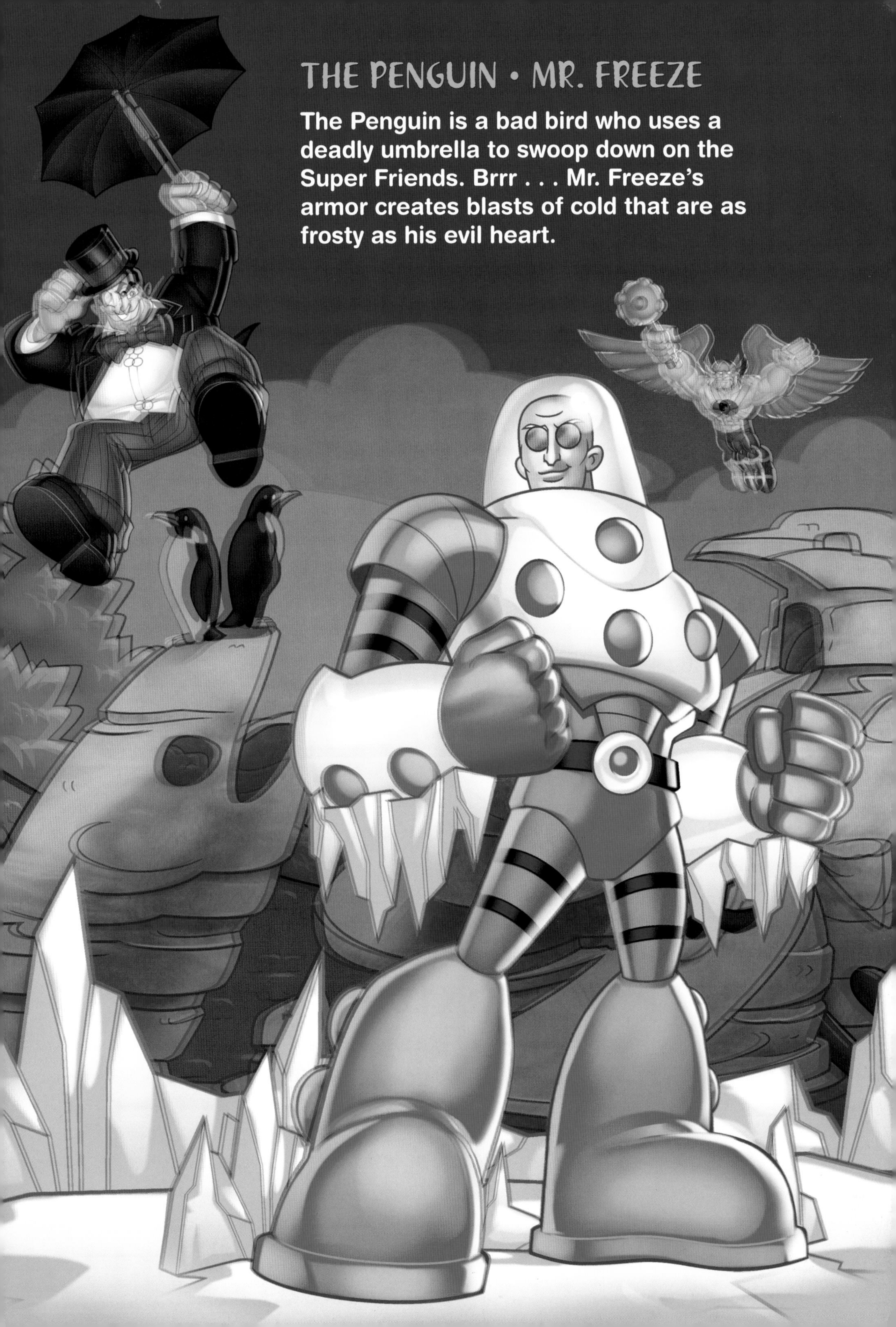

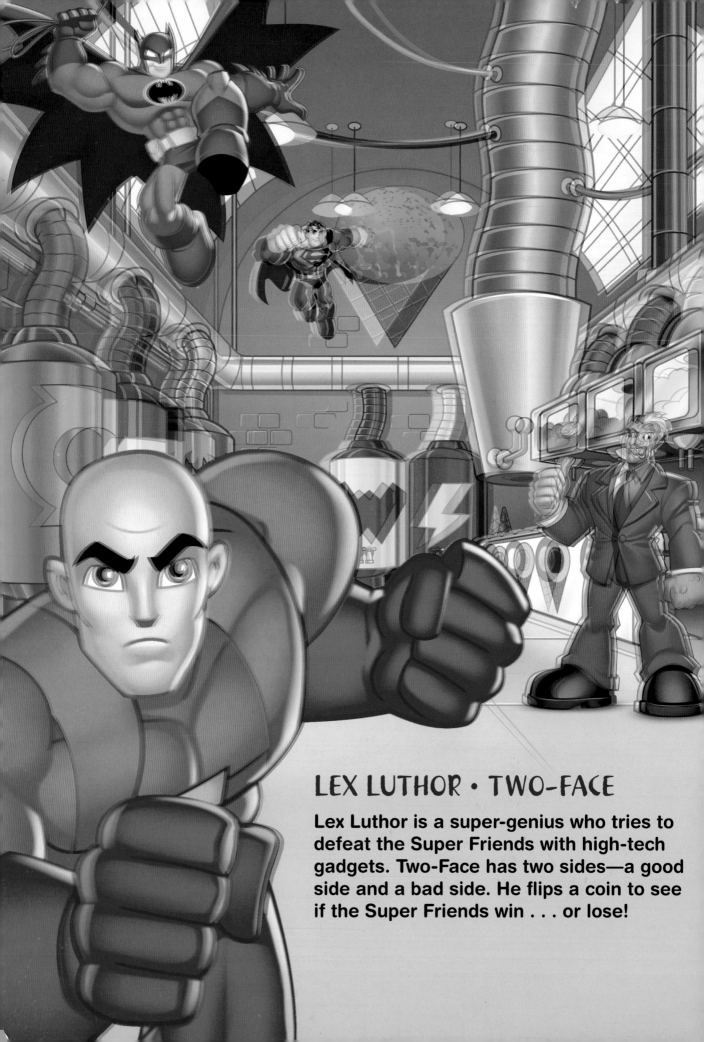

LEX LUTHOR • TWO-FACE

Lex Luthor is a super-genius who tries to defeat the Super Friends with high-tech gadgets. Two-Face has two sides—a good side and a bad side. He flips a coin to see if the Super Friends win . . . or lose!